NURSE!!

A CIP catalogue record for this book
is available from the British Library
ISBN 0-370-31539-1

Copyright © Sarah Garland 1990
Printed and bound in Hong Kong for
The Bodley Head Children's Books
an imprint of The Random Century Group Ltd
20 Vauxhall Bridge Road, London SW1V 2SA

First published in Great Britain in 1990

Reprinted 1991

For Rosie and the children at Elms Road.

GOING TO PLAYSCHOOL

Sarah Garland

THE BODLEY HEAD
London

This is playschool

and here's your peg.

Time for a game,

then pouring sand,

rolling out pastry,

painting pictures,

dressing up and

undressing.

A rest and a drink of juice,

and outside to play.

Look at the rabbit!

Coats on, boots on,

but where's the rabbit?